A Very Special Friend

Dorothy Hoffman Levi • Illustrations by Ethel Gold

Kendall Green Publications
Gallaudet University Press
Washington, D.C.

Kendall Green Publications
An imprint of Gallaudet University Press
Washington, DC 20002

Illustrations ©1989 by Ethel Gold
Published 1989
Printed in the United States of America

Library of Congress Cataloging-in-Publication Data

Levi, Dorothy, 1942-
    A very special friend.

    Summary: In search of a friend her own age, six-year-old Frannie meets Laura, who
is deaf, and learns sign language from her.
    [1. Deaf—Fiction. 2. Physically handicapped—Fiction. 3. Friendship—Fiction] I.
Title.
PZ7.L576Ve 1989   [E]   88-33410
ISBN 0-930323-55-6

Gallaudet University is an equal opportunity employer/educational institution. Programs and
services offered by Gallaudet University receive substantial financial support from the U.S.
Department of Education.

For my parents, Sid and Ethel Hoffman, and my children, Kara, Heather, and Ron, who always believed in me and my dream. ■

Frannie was a little girl who didn't know how to smile. She was sad because she had no friends.

She lived in a new yellow house with her mother, her father, and her puppy Sammy. But she felt lonely. Everybody smiled at the girl with curly brown hair that bounced when she walked and green eyes that sparkled like emeralds when she talked. But *she* never smiled back.

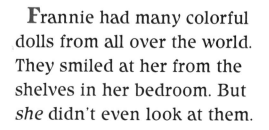

Frannie had many colorful dolls from all over the world. They smiled at her from the shelves in her bedroom. But *she* didn't even look at them.

Each day Frannie rode her shiny red bicycle down the block looking everywhere for that boy or girl who would be her special friend. Many children lived in Frannie's neighborhood. Some were too big. They didn't want to play with a little girl like Frannie. Others were too little. They didn't even know how to play games. No one was just the right size.

One day when Frannie was riding her bicycle very fast pretending that she was driving a fire engine, she saw a big truck pull up to a house down the street.

"What is happening?" she asked her mother.

"That is a moving truck. Soon we will have a new family on our block," her mother answered.

"Maybe there will be a little boy or girl my age," said Frannie excitedly. She *almost* smiled, but not quite.

Frannie got off her bicycle and walked toward the truck. Then she closed her eyes, crossed her fingers and toes, and wished very hard for a very special friend. When she opened her eyes again, she saw the movers taking out furniture. She saw a large, green, striped sofa; comfortable leather chairs; and a big bed.

And then Frannie began to smile. She felt all warm and happy inside because she saw a little bed that looked very much like hers. A minute later a car stopped right behind the truck. A mother, father, and a little girl just Frannie's size stepped out. The little girl waved when she saw Frannie. She had short blond hair that swirled when she walked, blue eyes that glowed like a summer sky, and a big happy smile.

"Hi," said Frannie.
The new girl said nothing.
Frannie waited and then said, "Hi," a little louder.
The new girl said something, but Frannie couldn't understand her.

Then she did something strange. When she saw that Frannie didn't understand her, instead of repeating what she said, she moved her hands. The new girl touched her forehead with her right hand and then smiled.

Puzzled, Frannie looked at the girl and said in a very loud voice, "I'm Frannie." The new girl looked friendly. She acted friendly. But Frannie couldn't understand what she was doing.

This time, she moved both hands, tapping her right hand on top of her left hand. And then she wiggled her fingers strangely, making different shapes. They looked like this:

Just then, the little girl's mother came over and said, "This is Laura. She can't hear you. She is deaf."

"What is she doing with her fingers?" Frannie asked.

"She is talking to you," Laura's mother answered.

"What is she saying?" Frannie wanted to know.

"She is saying, 'Hello, my name is Laura,' in sign language. She spelled her name for you. Many deaf people talk by using sign language and spelling words with their fingers. Sometimes they make up signs so they don't have to spell their names all the time. My daughter's name sign is an *L* making a big smile."

Frannie looked at Laura's mother. She looked at Laura. And then she began to cry. As fast as she could, she ran home and closed the door of her room. All the dolls were still there smiling. Frannie felt lonelier and sadder than ever.

Frannie's mother knocked on the door and said gently, "Please let me in, Frannie."

When Frannie opened the door, her mother asked, "Why did you run away from your new friend?"

"She is not my friend," said Frannie. "How can she ever be my friend? Friends talk to each other. They tell each other everything. Laura doesn't talk like me. We can't talk to each other."

"**O**f course you can," her mother said, holding Frannie very close. And then she gave Frannie a big hug and kiss. "Friends talk to each other in many different ways," she explained. "Sometimes they don't even need words at all. You and Laura can talk to each other in special ways. You can understand each other in spoken words and in sign language. Why don't you ask Laura to teach you some signs?"

"I can't. I'm too embarrassed," Frannie said.

She looked out the window and saw Laura wheeling her doll carriage up and down the block all alone. Sammy saw her, too. Suddenly, he ran toward Laura and, in a flash, he jumped into the carriage.

Laura laughed. Frannie laughed. Even Sammy looked as if he were laughing. Frannie banged on the window and yelled, "Laura, I'm coming." She ran out of the house and waved to Laura. Laura looked up and began to smile. Her smile grew bigger and bigger until her face looked like a balloon about to burst.

When Frannie was right beside her, Laura patted Sammy and signed, "Nice dog." Frannie smiled and copied her hand motions.

Both girls hugged Sammy and, before very long, they were also hugging each other. With her hands, Laura asked Frannie, "Will you be my friend?"

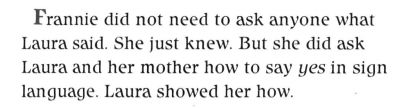

Frannie did not need to ask anyone what Laura said. She just knew. But she did ask Laura and her mother how to say *yes* in sign language. Laura showed her how.

All summer long, the two happy, always smiling, girls played together. Laura taught Frannie many signs. After a few weeks, Frannie could understand many of Laura's signs and the way she talked, and Laura could understand what Frannie signed to her. The girls had fun talking in two languages.

On their very last day of summer vacation, Frannie and Laura talked only about school and what a good time they would have that year. Over and over again, they said and signed, "School tomorrow!" That night, they went to bed very early, but neither girl could sleep. They were both too excited.

The next morning Frannie's mother took the best friends to school.
They saw many children standing outside talking and playing.

Frannie knew some of the boys and girls. They came over to say hello, and pretty soon, Frannie was surrounded by her old friends. But Laura stood all alone. Her big smile got smaller and smaller until, finally, it just disappeared.

Then suddenly Frannie turned toward Laura and brought her into the circle. She gave Laura a big hug. Frannie said to all her school friends in a loud clear voice and in sign language, "I want you to meet Laura, my very special friend."

Some Signs
You Can Learn

The directions for making signs are written for right-handed people. Use your right hand for the one-handed signs. If you are left-handed, substitute *left* wherever the directions say *right*. For example: to make the sign for *dog*, pat your right thigh with your right hand. If you are left-handed, pat your left thigh with your left hand.■

American Manual Alphabet

 A

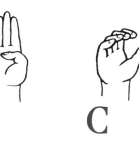 B

C

D

E

F

G

 H

I

 J

 K

 L

 M

 N

O

 P

Q

 R

 S

T

 U

 V

W

 X

Y

 Z

dog

Pat your right thigh twice.

hello

Move your hand straight out from your forehead.

name

Tap your right index and middle fingers across your left index and middle fingers.

nice

Slide your right hand off your left palm.

school

Place your right hand across your left palm and clap twice.

tomorrow

Touch your cheek with your right thumb and twist your hand forward.

water

Make a *W* and tap your chin twice.

yes

Bend your fist up and down a few times.

friend

Hook your right index finger over your left index finger. Then turn your hands over and hook your left index finger over your right index finger.

Dorothy Hoffman Levi is a writer and teacher. She lives in New York City with her three children. Her comments on contemporary life have been published in several newspapers, including *The New York Times*. She received a grant from the New York State Department of Education and a scholarship from *The New York Times*. This is her first children's book. She is currently working on a novel. ∎